MY BOOK of SPECIAL DAYS

a FRANCES HOOK picture book

with stories by MARIAN BENNETT

STANDARD PUBLISHING
Cincinnati, Ohio 3049

To my grandson, Brian

ISBN: 0-87239-156-6

© 1977 by The STANDARD PUBLISHING Company, Cincinnati, Ohio,
a division of STANDEX INTERNATIONAL Corporation. Printed in U.S.A.

Presented to

____

by

____

JESUS LIVES AGAIN

Jesus was dead.

His friends were very sad. Jesus, the kindest, most loving person they had ever known, was dead.

Jesus had let His enemies hang Him on a cross. They had made fun of Him and spit in His face, but He didn't say a word to them.

Then Jesus had died. Many terrible things had happened. The sun was covered so that it was as dark as night. The earth had shaken and rumbled.

Then His friends had taken Jesus' body and placed it in a tomb. His friends went home. The next day they rested. They probably cried some more. Their dearest friend was dead.

But early on the first day of the new week, something wonderful happened. An angel came and rolled away the stone that had been placed in front of the tomb. Then Jesus walked out of the tomb. He wasn't dead anymore. He was alive. Jesus, God's Son, was alive!

Many of Jesus' friends saw Him that first day. He walked with them and ate with them. How happy they all were!

Finally, after forty days, Jesus went back to Heaven to live with His Father. He is there now, waiting for all those who obey Him.

Jesus is alive!

Story from Matthew 27 and Luke 24

F. Hook

NEW LIFE

"Look, Mommy! My tulip has a big flower on it. Isn't it pretty?"

Mother came to look at the beautiful big tulip. "That is a very pretty tulip, Brian," she said.

"Where did the tulip come from, Mommy?"

"Remember when we bought the dry brown bulbs and planted them last fall?" his mother explained. "You helped me dig holes in the garden and put the bulbs in, then we covered them with dirt and gave them a drink of water."

"I remember that. I liked the feel of the dirt when I patted it down on the bulb. I filled the sprinkling can for you, didn't I?"

"Yes," Brian's mother answered, "you were a big help!"

"What happened to the bulbs last winter when we had snow on the ground?" Brian asked.

"Well," his mother continued, "they were buried all winter long in the ground. When the sun came out and warmed them enough they began to grow. First a little green tip came up above the ground. Remember when you found that? I told you it would grow to be a tall tulip someday, and that you would have to wait and watch for a few weeks."

Waiting and watching had been hard for Brian. He had gone out every day to see how much the tulip had grown. He thought it would never grow big. Then one day Brian had found a bud on the tulip. Now it was a beautiful flower. Mommy had been right.

The little brown bulb had been buried just like the body of Jesus had been so many years ago. Then, just as Jesus came back to life, so the little tulip came to life from the dead bulb.

Whenever you see a beautiful flower growing in the garden, remember how Jesus came back to life. And some day, we will have a new life, just as the little tulip bulb did. There's new life in Jesus.

TIMOTHY AND HIS MOTHER

Timothy had a loving mother named Eunice, and a dear grandmother named Lois. Both his mother and his grandmother spent much time with Timothy, telling him stories about Bible men such as Noah, Joseph, David, and Daniel. Timothy loved to hear these stories. He would sit on his mother's lap for hours and listen as she read from the Bible-scroll. Timothy knew that the words in the Bible-scroll came from God.

The story of David the shepherd boy was probably one of Timothy's favorites. He hoped God would help him to be brave just as He had helped David.

Eunice had first heard God's Word from her mother, Lois. Now she wanted Timothy to know these same words. Eunice also knew she must set a good example for her son. Her mother had done this for her.

Many years later, the apostle Paul would write a letter to Timothy and say, "I remember the great faith that is in you that was first of all in your grandmother, Lois, and then in your mother, Eunice." Paul knew that Timothy's faith had started when he was a boy sitting on his mother's lap, listening to the words from the Bible-scroll.

When Timothy grew up he became a preacher of the Word of God. He traveled with Paul and helped with his work. Because of what his mother and grandmother had taught him, Timothy was able to teach others God's Word.

Story from 2 Timothy

MOTHER'S DAY

Kathy and Kenny wanted to do something special for their mother this year for Mother's Day. They talked to their Dad about this, and they decided that it would be nice to cook dinner for Mother.

On Saturday, Daddy, Kathy, and Kenny went to the store and bought the groceries they would need. The children baked a cake, with Dad's help, then each one licked a beater when the frosting was finished. Cooking was fun!

Mother said that it was the best dinner she had ever tasted. Kathy and Kenny thought the potatoes needed more salt, and the gravy had lumps, but they agreed that the cake was good!

When everyone had finished eating, Kathy and Kenny took Mother by the hand and led her to the porch. Then the children brought out the gift they had bought for Mother. It was a beautiful violet plant covered with purple blooms. As Kathy held the plant, Kenny gave his mother a big kiss. Mother took the plant and smiled. There was a little tear in her eye. "Children, this has been the best Mother's Day I've ever had!" she exclaimed.

Kathy and Kenny felt nice and warm inside as they went in the house to help Dad clean up after the dinner. Now they understood the Bible words, "It is more blessed to give than to receive." In fact, they didn't even mind doing the dishes.

THE LOST SON

Jesus told the story of a father and son. One day, the son came to his father and asked for his part of the father's money. Then the son left home and went far away. He used all his money trying to have a good time. When the money was gone, his friends left him and he had no place to live and no food to eat.

The young man had to take a job feeding hogs. He was so hungry he wanted to eat the food the hogs ate. Then he began to think about what he had done. "What a fool I've been! I made my father feel sad by leaving home. I wasted my time and money on parties. Now here I am in the pen with hogs." He decided to go home and tell his father how sorry he was.

The young man hurried home. When he was almost home, he saw a man running to meet him. It was his father! The son ran into his father's arms. They both cried tears of joy.

"Father," the son said, "I'm not good enough to be called your son any more. Please make me just a hired servant in your house."

The father called his servants to bring good clothes for his son, a ring for his finger, and shoes for his feet. Then the father told the servants to prepare a great dinner to celebrate his son's return.

"My son is home! He was lost and now he is found! This is a time to be very happy!"

Jesus showed us in this story how much a father loves his children. Even though his son had been wrong, the father forgave him and welcomed him home. Jesus wanted us to know that God, our heavenly Father, loves us the way our earthly fathers do, only much more than that. He is always willing to forgive us when we tell Him we're sorry. God's love is wonderful!

Story from Luke 15:11-24

HOOK

FATHER'S DAY

Kathy and Kenny had been saving their money for a Father's Day gift for their dad. They had just enough money to buy him a pair of socks. They looked at their gift as it lay there in the box.

Finally Kathy spoke. "A pair of socks isn't much of a gift for Daddy, is it?"

Kenny agreed with his sister. "I wish we could buy him something that would show how much we love him!" exclaimed Kenny.

"We've got the best dad in the whole world, but how can we tell him that?" said Kathy sadly. Then she had an idea. "I know what we can do."

Kathy quickly wrote something on a piece of paper. Kenny, who couldn't read yet, looked at the paper, and then at Kathy. "What's that?" he asked.

"It says, 'I love you enough to help you clean the garage,' " said Kathy.

"Write one for me, too," Kenny said.

Kathy wrote again. " 'I love Dad enough to help him pull weeds in the garden for one whole week.' How does that sound?"

Kenny liked that idea. Then the children put their notes in with the socks and wrapped the package.

"Happy Father's Day!" both children said as they handed their dad his gift the next morning.

Daddy opened the box and said he liked the socks. Then he read the notes. He smiled at Kenny and Kathy. "That's the nicest kind of gift you can give—yourselves. Only *you* can give that. Thanks, both of you," he said as he gave each of them a big hug.

THE FEAST OF BOOTHS

Rebekah had been helping her mother prepare food all day. As each dish of food was ready, her mother carefully placed it in a basket. Rebekah wondered why her mother was doing this. Were they going on a long trip again? Rebekah could remember when they had made the long trip from Babylon to Jerusalem. They had spent many weeks traveling and she had grown tired.

"Mother, where are we taking this food?" she asked.

"We are going to take it to the rooftop," answered her mother.

Rebekah loved to play on the flat roof of their house. Sometimes she even slept there when the house was too hot. But why were they taking all this food up there?

Just then Rebekah's father and two little brothers came home. They had brought many tree branches. Rebekah watched her father as he began to build a shelter on their rooftop. "Father, why are you doing that?" she asked.

"Well," began her father, "I'm building a booth for us to live in for the next week. Do you remember when Ezra the priest read to us from God's Word? We learned that God wanted us to keep a feast each year to remind us of His goodness. He has given us good crops for food. We must tell Him thanks for that. Also, He was good to our people when He led them through the wilderness many years ago into the promised land—the land we live in now. We must never forget this. So, for seven days, all of our people are going to live in booths just as they once did in the wilderness. Each day we shall tell God 'Thank You' for all He has done for us."

Rebekah was excited. She knew that this was going to be a happy time for her family. Truly, God had been good to them. She wanted to thank Him.

Story from Nehemiah 8

THANKSGIVING DAY

"Thank You for the food, and for all the other blessings You've given us. In Jesus' name, amen." So ended Daddy's prayer for the Thanksgiving dinner. Then the turkey was carved, plates were passed, and everyone began to eat. How good everything tasted!

As the family ate, Daddy reminded them of the first Thanksgiving that was held when the Pilgrims lived in America.

"They had had a very hard winter. But in the spring they planted crops, and by fall there was a good harvest. The Pilgrims were truly thankful to God for all they had," said Daddy.

"The women must have had a hard time preparing all that food without a sink, or stove, or even running water. I'm surely glad I have a nice kitchen to work in," added Mother.

"I wish I could have been a Pilgrim," Jimmy decided. "Maybe I could have gone hunting and fishing instead of going to school."

"Remember," Beth said, "you would have had lots of hard work, like helping in the field, chopping wood, carrying water, and . . ."

"And don't forget," reminded Billy, "you wouldn't have had a bike to ride or TV to watch."

"There weren't parks to play ball in, or even many children to play with," added Beth.

"No, the Pilgrims didn't have any of these things that we enjoy. But they had some things that were more important," said Mother. "They had their lives, they had enough food, they had their Indian friends, and they had freedom. And for all this they were thankful. Since we have so much more than they had, how much more thankful we ought to be, not only today, but every day of our lives."

READING GOD'S WORD

Every morning and every evening Father took the big scroll and began with these words: "Hear, O Israel: The Lord our God is one Lord."

Joshua, Benjie, and little Sarah listened quietly as Father continued to read. They had been taught since they were babies that they must be very quiet while Father spoke these words.

Joshua looked over Father's shoulder. "What are all those strange marks?" he asked after his father was finished.

"Those are words—God's words," replied his father.

"Did God write them with His own hand?" Joshua wanted to know.

"No," answered Father. "Long ago, God told men what to write, and they put down the words for us. Some of those words tells us how we are to live. Some of them tell us what is good and what is bad. The words I have been reading tell us how important it is for us to know God's Word."

"I wish I could read the words the way you do, Father."

"Josh, you are getting old enough to learn. Some day Benjie will learn, too. Then you will be able to tell others what God's Word says," explained Father.

Joshua was glad that he was big enough to learn to read. Perhaps Father would let him read from the big scroll so Mother, Benjie, and Sarah could hear God's Word.

Story from Deuteronomy 6

THE BIBLE, GOD'S TRUTH

"Come, children, it's time for devotions," called Mother.

Jennifer put down the book she had been reading. Family devotion time was an important time in her home. She knew Mom and Dad expected her to come when they called.

Jason put away the trucks he'd been playing with and went downstairs.

"Whose turn is it to choose the Bible verses to be read?" asked Daddy.

"I believe it is my turn tonight," answered Mother, "and I'd like for you to read Psalm 100. I always feel good when I hear that one."

Daddy began to read: "Make a joyful noise unto the Lord," and ended with, "and his truth endureth to all generations."

As soon as Daddy finished reading, they all took turns praying.

After prayers were over Jason asked, "Do you suppose people in Jesus' day read that psalm?"

"I'm sure they did," answered Daddy. "The last part of the psalm tells us something important. God's truth, the Bible, will last to all generations. That means that what was true when God gave it to man was true a hundred years later, a thousand years later, and even today. The Bible will still be true when you are grown, and when your children read it."

Jennifer thought about this. It made her feel very good to know that she could always trust God's Word to be true, no matter what others might say or do. Jennifer was glad that her family took time to read the Bible, God's truth.

THE BIRTH OF JESUS

The journey from Nazareth to Bethlehem had been long and tiresome. Joseph had been so kind and patient to let Mary rest often along the way. Now she could see the lights of the town in the distance. Soon they would have a room where they could rest.

As Mary and Joseph entered the little town—the city of David—they were met by great crowds of people. Everyone was trying to find a room. Always, the answer was "No." Then Joseph met a man who said they could sleep in his stable. "At least there is some clean hay to make a bed," Joseph told Mary. She was too tired to answer.

Joseph spread their blankets on a fresh pile of hay so that Mary could lie down. Joseph knew that Mary needed a place to rest, for her baby would be born very soon.

And that night, there in the stable, Mary's baby was born. They named Him Jesus, just as the angel had said, for this was a very special baby—God's Son. He had been promised for so many years, and now at last He had come to earth, not born in the palace of a king, but in a stable, among the animals.

Just as all new mothers did, Mary looked lovingly at her newborn son. How beautiful He was! How she loved Him! All too soon she would have to share Him with the rest of the world, but for this moment He was hers. How she would remember these days!

Story from Matthew 1:21 and Luke 2:1-7

THE NATIVITY SCENE

For days Amy had been asking her big sister, Karen, to take her to see the nativity scene that was in the churchyard. One day, when school was out, Karen agreed to take her. The girls put on warm coats and hats and walked down the street. Amy was excited!

There were many children at the nativity scene. Some had come to pet the live animals—the woolly sheep, the cows, and the little donkey. Amy liked the animals.

Amy looked at the figure of the pretty young mother. Amy decided that Mary looked very kind and loving. Then Amy looked at the tall figure of the man. She asked, "Karen, who is the man standing by Mary?"

Karen answered, "That is Joseph, Mary's husband. He helped take care of baby Jesus."

Then Amy looked at the tiny baby. "Why is He lying in that funny box? Where is His crib?"

"Baby Jesus was born in a stable. There wasn't any crib, so Mary laid Him in a manger filled with hay," Karen explained.

"Why would God let His Son be born in a stable?" wondered Amy.

"God planned it that way," was the answer.

"He must have loved people very much to give His Son to us."

"That's right, Amy. God loves us more than we'll ever know."